MATCHMAKER 911

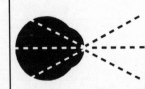

This Large Print Book carries the
Seal of Approval of N.A.V.H.

MATCHMAKER 911

WANDA E. BRUNSTETTER

THORNDIKE PRESS
A part of Gale, Cengage Learning

GALE
CENGAGE Learning

Detroit • New York • San Francisco • New Haven, Conn • Waterville, Maine • London

GALE
CENGAGE Learning®

LIBRARY OF CONGRESS CATALOGING-IN-PUBLICATION DATA

Brunstetter, Wanda E.
    Matchmaker 911 / by Wanda E. Brunstetter. — Large print ed.
        p. cm. — (Thorndike Press large print Christian romance) (Love finds a Way; #3)
        ISBN-13: 978-1-4104-4756-2 (hardcover)
        ISBN-10: 1-4104-4756-1 (hardcover)
        1. Large type books. 2. Widows—Fiction. I. Title. II. Title: Matchmaker nine-one-one.
    PS3602.R864M38 2012
    813'.6—dc23   2012011470

Published in 2012 by arrangement with Barbour Publishing, Inc.

Printed in the United States of America
1 2 3 4 5 6 7 16 15 14 13 12

To my daughter-in-law, Jean,
whose first career was barbering.

CHAPTER 1

"Ya know what?" croaked an aged, gravelly-sounding voice. "I was six months old before I even saw the light of day!"

In the past four years of cutting customers' hair, Wendy Campbell had listened to more ridiculous jokes and boring stories than she cared to admit. Clyde Baxter sat in her antique barber's chair, and she was quite certain she was about to hear another joke or two from him. Barbering was her chosen profession, and as long as it wasn't an off-color joke, she would play along.

"Why's that, Clyde?" Wendy prompted, knowing if she didn't make some kind of response, the elderly man would probably tell her anyway.

"Well, darlin', my mother, God rest her soul, was a bit nearsighted. So the poor woman kept on diaperin' the wrong end!"

Wendy's muffled groan did nothing to deter the amicable man, and with no further encouragement, he continued. "Now, I don't want to say I was an ugly baby or anything, but I hear tell that the doctor who brought me into this ol' world took one look at my homely mug and promptly made a citizen's arrest on my daddy!" At this remark, Clyde roared with laughter.

Wendy grimaced. The joke was respectable enough, but thanks to Clyde's interruptions by moving around each time he laughed, this haircut was taking much longer than it should. It was only ten o'clock, and she still had several more clients scheduled in the next two hours — including four-year-old Benny Jensen, the kid who hated haircuts and liked to kick and scream. That didn't take into account any walk-ins who might happen by either.

Wendy could hardly wait for lunchtime when she could run home, grab a quick bite to eat, and check up on her father. At least *Dad* had sense enough not to tell a bunch of lame wisecracks and off-color stories. Wendy didn't mind cutting hair, and now that Dad couldn't work, she certainly needed the money. There were days like today though, when she wondered if a woman working in a predominately man's world was really such a good idea.

"Why, I'll never forget the day I graduated from grammar school," Clyde continued, with a silly grin plastered on his seventy-year-old, weathered face. "I tell you, I was so nervous I could hardly shave!" The old man laughed so hard this time that his whole body shook, and he had tears running down his wrinkled cheeks.

Wendy rolled her eyes toward the plastered ceiling and feigned a smile. "You'd better quit laughing and hold still, Clyde. If you don't, it might be your ear that comes off and not those sideburns you've finally decided to

10

part with."

Clyde slapped his knee and let out another loud guffaw, ending it on a definite pig snort. "Tell ya what, honey, you could probably take my ear clean off, and it wouldn't make much never mind to me. I can only hear outa one ear anyways, and I ain't rightly sure which one that is!"

Without making any reply, Wendy took a few more snips and followed them with a quick once-over on the back of Clyde's stubbly neck with her clippers. She dusted him off with a soft-bristled brush and announced, "There you go, Clyde. That ought to hold you for at least another month."

Wendy was already moving toward her antiquated cash register, which had to be manually opened by the use of a handle on one side. Due to the hour, she sincerely hoped her joke-telling client would take the hint and move on.

Clyde finally stood up and ambled slowly over to where she stood, smiling through clenched teeth and waiting impatiently for him to pay. "You sure ain't much for fun today, are you, little lady?"

Before Wendy could think of an intelligent reply, Clyde added, "Nothin' like your old man, that's for sure. Why, good old Wayne used to tease like crazy all of the time. He could tell some jokes that just kept ya in stitches, too!"

Clyde appeared thoughtful, with a faraway look clouding his aging eyes. "I sure do miss that guy. It's been two years now since he took a razor to my chin or shortened my ears a few inches with them clippers of his. Such a downright shame that your daddy can't cut hair no more."

Wendy nodded, causing her short, blond curls to bounce. "Dad's been battling arthritis a long time. After two knee replacements and even having the joints in his fingers surgically repaired, I'm afraid the disease has finally gotten the best of him. He hardly gets out of the house anymore, unless it's to go to the hospital for his regular physical therapy appointments. Once in a while, he still stops by here, if the weather is good enough and he's not in too much pain. He likes to sit right there and reminisce." She pointed with the tip of her scissors to her dad's old barbering chair in the corner of her early American shop and swallowed the impulse to shed a few tears.

Clyde clicked his tongue noisily. "Wayne sure could cut hair."

Wendy brushed some of Clyde's prickly gray hair off the front of her blue cotton smock. "Yes, he was a great partner. Even when all Dad could do was sit and give me instructions, he taught me a whole lot that I never learned in barber's school."

The old man gave Wendy a quick wink. "Don't get me wrong, little lady. I wasn't tryin' to say you can't cut hair. For a little whip of a gal, you're a real whiz at scissor snippin'."

"Thanks — I think," Wendy said with a grin as Clyde handed her eight dollars for his haircut. She pulled sharply on the handle of the cash register, dropped the bills inside, then snapped the drawer shut. Wendy moved toward the front door, assuming Clyde would follow.

"You know what a little gal like yourself really needs?" Clyde asked, obviously not in much of a hurry to leave.

Wendy drew in a deep breath then let it out in a rush. "No, Clyde, what *do* I need?"

Playfully, the old man poked her on the arm and laughed. "You need a man in your life — that's what you need. Maybe someone like that good-looking fellow Gabe Hunter."

Wendy bit down firmly on her bottom lip. She was trying so hard to be patient with Clyde, but if he didn't head for home soon, there was a good chance she might say something she would probably regret. Clyde didn't understand what it was like for her. No one did, really. She had a deep hurt from the past that affected her response to men. Having so many guys at the shop trying to make a play for her only made things worse.

"Dad is the only man I need," she affirmed, opening the front door and letting in a blast of chilly air. "I have all I can do just to take care of him and keep this little barbershop running."

Clyde shrugged and slipped into the heavy jacket he'd hung on one of the wooden wall pegs near the door. "Suit yourself, girlie, but I think a little romance might be just the ticket."

With that, he crammed his hands into his pockets and strolled out of the shop.

After Wendy swept the floor clean of hair one more time and said good-bye to her final customer of the morning, she leaned heavily against the door and let out a low moan. Her stomach rumbled with hunger, and a feeling of weariness settled over her like a heavy blanket of fog. She licked her lips in anticipation of going home, where she could have something to eat, prop her feet up for a while, and get in a short visit with the only man in her life. Dad always seemed so eager to hear what was going on at the barbershop, often plying her with questions about who came in today, what they said or did, and whether Wendy was sure she could handle things on her own. Her father seemed to pride himself on being in total control. He'd run a barbershop for more than twenty years and sent her to barber's school so she could be his partner in this small Northwest town.

However, there were at least two things Wendy knew he hadn't been able to control. First, he'd had no control over his wife's untimely death, when she was killed by a drunk driver nearly ten years ago. That terrible accident had left him a widower with a young daughter to care for. Yet in all these years, she'd never heard him complain. Nor had her fifty-year-old father been able to control the doctor's diagnosis of severe rheumatoid arthritis many years ago. Wendy knew it had been a terrible blow, especially when he'd tried so hard to keep on working. Eventually, he had to turn the shop over to her and retire his barbering shears.

"Why did it have to happen? Sometimes life seems so unfair," Wendy lamented as she reached for her coat. As she closed the door, a chilling wind blew against Wendy's face, stinging her eyes and causing her nose to run. "I'll be so glad when spring finally comes," she murmured. "At least then Dad will feel more like getting out."

Wendy's house was just a block from Campbell's Barbershop, so she always walked to and from work. The exercise did her good, and it only took a few minutes to get there. As usual, Wendy found the front door of their modest, brick-faced home unlocked. In a town as small as Plumers, everyone knew each other. The crime rate was almost nonexistent. Leaving doors and windows unlocked was one of the fringe benefits of small-town living.

Dad sat in his vibrating, heat-activated recliner, staring out the living room window. He offered Wendy a warm smile when she came though the door. Tipping his head, the dark hair now thinning and streaked with gray, he asked the proverbial question. "How's business?"

"About the same as usual, Dad," Wendy answered. "How was your morning?"

"About the same as usual." He chuckled. "Except for one thing."

She draped her coat over the back of the couch and took a seat. "Oh, and what was that?"

"Clyde Baxter phoned. We had

quite a talk."

Wendy leaned her head back against the cushions. "Clyde was in the shop this morning. Of course, I'm sure he told you."

He lifted himself from the recliner and reached for his walking cane. "Clyde didn't tell any of his off-color jokes, I hope. I'll have a talk with him about that, if it's still a problem."

Wendy shook her head. "He was a perfect gentleman today. Just told a few clean jokes." She propped her feet on the coffee table and sighed deeply, choosing not to mention the fact that the elderly man's stories were repeats from other times he'd been in the shop. "So what else did Clyde have to say to you, Dad?"

"He thinks you need a man in your life," he said, grunting as he sat down beside her.

Wendy gritted her teeth. "Clyde doesn't know what he's talking about."

Dad reached out to lay a gnarled hand on her jean-clad knee. "You do spend most of your time running the barbershop and taking care of me. A young woman needs a social life. She needs —"

"You're all I need, Dad," Wendy interrupted. She gave his hand a few gentle pats, then abruptly stood. "I don't know about you, but I'm starving. What would you like for lunch?"

He shrugged. "I'm not all that hungry. I thought we could talk awhile."

"If it's about me finding a man, you can forget it." Wendy started for the kitchen but turned back just before she reached the adjoining door. "Dad, I know you have another physical therapy appointment this afternoon. Would you like me to close the shop and drive you over to the hospital in Grangely?"

Dad shook his head. "I've already called People for People, and they're sending a van out around one thirty."

Wendy nodded. "Okay, if that's what you want." She closed her eyes and inhaled sharply. At least she had managed to successfully change the subject. She headed for the kitchen, wondering, *Now why does everyone suddenly think I need a man?*

Paramedic Kyle Rogers and his partner, Steve, had just brought an elderly woman to the hospital. She'd been doing some laundry and slipped go-

23

ing down the basement steps. The physicians determined a possible broken hip. Kyle left the woman in the emergency room and was heading to the cafeteria. Steve was parking their vehicle and planned to join him for a much-needed lunch after he checked their supplies.

I sure hope we don't get any more calls for a while, Kyle thought. *It's only three o'clock, but I'm completely beat!* The morning hours had been full, with several 911 calls coming from the three smaller towns surrounding Grangely. This afternoon they'd already had two local emergencies. Kyle would be the first to admit that the life of a paramedic was often grueling. A few good men and women burned out even before they reached their midthirties. Some became harsh and callous from witnessing so many maladies, too.

One of the worst tragedies Kyle had ever seen was a young college student who'd committed suicide by jumping out his dorm room window. The mere image of the distorted man made him cringe. Kyle knew he would never be able to handle such abhorrent things without Christ supporting him.

As he entered the cafeteria, Kyle saw a middle-aged man using a cane with one hand, trying to balance a tray filled with a cup of coffee and a donut with the other. It looked as if the poor fellow was about to lose the whole thing, as it tipped precariously this way and that. Before Kyle could respond, the cup tilted slightly, spilling some of the hot coffee onto the tray.

"Here, let me help you," he said to the red-faced man. "Where do you plan to sit? I'll set the tray on the table."

The man nodded toward the closest table. "Right there's fine."

Kyle put the tray down and pulled out a chair. "Here you go, sir."

The man's hand trembled as he reached it toward Kyle. "The name's Wayne Campbell, and I sure do appreciate your help, young man."

Kyle smiled warmly, and being careful not to apply too much pressure, he shook the arthritic hand briefly. "I'm Kyle Rogers, and I'm just glad I happened to be in the right place at the right time." Unconsciously, he reached up to place one finger against the small *WWJD* button he wore on his shirt pocket. Just thinking about the man's gnarled hands filled him with compassion. *I bet those hands used to be hardworking. Probably cradled a baby at one time, or maybe stroked a wife's cheeks with ease. The poor man has lost so much normal function that he couldn't even balance a tray with one hand.*

"Are all paramedics this helpful?" Wayne questioned, breaking into Kyle's thoughts.

Kyle shrugged and ran his fingers through his thick dark hair. "I can't speak for all paramedics, but I try to do whatever God asks of me."

Wayne nodded and took the offered seat. "You're welcome to join me. In fact, I'd appreciate the company."

Kyle nodded. "Sure, why not? My

partner's meeting me here for a late lunch, so if you don't mind sitting with a couple of tired paramedics, we'd be happy to share your table."

Wayne smiled in response. "No problem a'tall. I just finished with physical therapy and was planning to gulp down a cup of coffee and inhale a fattening donut before I head for home."

"I guess I'll go get myself a sandwich," Kyle said. "How about if I get you another cup of coffee?"

Wayne reached into his jacket pocket to retrieve his wallet. "Here, let me give you some money, then."

Kyle waved the gesture aside. "Don't worry about it." He grinned and moved over to the snack bar before the older man had a chance to respond.

A short time later, Kyle joined Wayne at the table, carrying a tray with one jelly donut, two cups of coffee, and a turkey club sandwich.

"You said this was your lunch?" Wayne asked as Kyle took a seat at the small table.

Kyle nodded. "We've been busy all day. There was no time to stop and eat at noon."

He bowed his head and offered a silent prayer of thanks for the food. When he opened his eyes and started to take a bite of sandwich, he noticed the arthritic man looking at him curiously.

"You rescue guys sure do keep long hours, don't you?" Wayne asked, slowly reaching for his cup of coffee.

"Sometimes our days can go anywhere from eight to twenty-four hours," Kyle admitted.

"Wow! That must be pretty hard on your family life."

Kyle shrugged. "I'm single, and it's probably a good thing, too. I don't have to worry about unpredictable hours causing my wife to burn dinner."

With a trembling hand, Wayne set the coffee cup down, spilling some as he did so. Kyle reached across the table and mopped up the mess with a few napkins.

Wayne frowned deeply. "Not only do I manage to nearly dump my whole tray, but I can't even drink a cup of coffee without spilling it all over the place." He shook his head and grumbled, "It's not bad enough that I've messed up my own life, but I'm afraid my only daughter will be strapped with me till the day I die."

Kyle glanced toward the cafeteria door. *Still no Steve. He must have gotten sidetracked along the way. Probably ran into one of those cute little nurses he likes to flirt with. Well, Lord, maybe my mission for the moment is to let this poor man unload some of his woes.* He gave Wayne Campbell his full attention. "What makes you think your daughter will be strapped with you?"

Wayne bit down on his bottom lip. "I'm a widower. My daughter, Wendy, not only works full-time, but has had the added burden of taking care of me for the last few years."

Kyle rubbed his forehead, praying for the right words of encouragement. "Does she complain about her situation?"

Wayne shrugged. "Not in so many words, but no matter how brave a front she puts on, I can tell she's unhappy." He bumped his hand against the edge of the table and winced. "Her attitude at home is fine, but at work — well, the last time I observed things, she seemed kind of testy."

Kyle patted Wayne's arm gently. "Maybe all your daughter needs is more love and understanding."

Wayne nodded. "You know, you might be right about that, son. I think Wendy could use a little bit of romance."

CHAPTER 2

Today was Tuesday, the first day of Wendy's workweek. She'd just closed up shop for lunch and was heading down the street toward home when the piercing whine of a siren blared through the air. It was all Wendy could do to keep from covering her ears and screaming. Sirens reminded her of that fateful day when her mother was killed. Clare Campbell had always been a crusader, and keeping the roadside free of litter was one of her many campaigns. She'd been walking just outside of town, picking up garbage as she went.

Wendy, only fifteen at the time, had been at the barbershop that Saturday morning, flirting with all the teenage boys who'd come in for a haircut and watching her father work. She heard the eerie sirens as they whizzed through Plumers, wondering what had happened. Sirens in their small town usually signaled some kind of serious mishap. A fire truck was sent from nearby Grangely for fires, and the paramedic vehicle came for accidents and serious ailments.

Wendy could still see the shocked expression on her dad's face when a police officer arrived at the barbershop and gave him the news that Mom had been hit by a car. Those sirens had been for her, only it was too little, too late. Clare Campbell was dead — killed instantly by a drunken driver who'd veered off the road.

The blaring sound drew closer now, pulling Wendy from the past and causing her to shiver. As the rescue vehicle flew past, she saw that it was the paramedic truck. Something serious must have happened. Someone would probably be taken to the hospital in Grangely.

Wendy began to walk a bit faster, broke into a cold sweat, then ran at full speed when she saw the vehicle stop in front of her house. It couldn't be! "Please, God, don't let anything happen to Dad," she prayed.

Two paramedics were already on the front porch when Wendy bounded up the stairs.

"It's open," she cried. "My father

never locks the front door."

One of the men turned to face her. "Did you make the call?"

Wendy shook her head. "No, I just got here." She yanked open the front door and dashed into the living room.

Her father sat slumped over on the floor. His cane, one leg, and both hands were badly tangled in a long piece of fishing line. A well-used rod and reel were connected to the other end of the line, lying at an odd angle against the front of the couch. The phone was on the floor by his hip. Its cord was wrapped around the twisted mess.

"Dad, what on earth happened?" Wendy dropped to her knees beside him, and the paramedics moved swiftly toward their patient.

"Mr. Campbell?" Kyle Rogers could hardly believe it. This was the same man he'd spoken to in the hospital cafeteria just last week.

"You remember me?" Wayne inquired as Kyle donned a pair of surgical gloves.

"Of course. We met at the Grangely Hospital last week," Kyle replied. "You seem to have a bit of a problem, sir. Are you hurt? You didn't get a fishhook stuck in your hand or anything, did you?"

Wayne groaned and shook his head. "I don't think so, but I'm so glad you're here. I was trying to tie some flies, but I sure made a mess of things, didn't I?" He glanced over at Wendy, who was white faced and wide eyed. "Don't look so serious, Wendy girl. I met one of these young

37

men at the hospital," he said, nodding toward Kyle. "He was nice enough to help me with some spilled coffee, and —"

"Dad, I'm concerned about you," Wendy interrupted. "How in the world did you get all tangled up like this?" Her forehead wrinkled. "And why didn't you call me instead of 911?"

Wayne shrugged. "Guess I thought you wouldn't know what to do." He glanced over at Kyle again. "Do you think you guys can get this stuff untangled? It's starting to cut off my circulation — what little I have left, that is," he added with a grimace.

Kyle turned to his partner. "Let's see what we can do to help the man, Steve."

As the two men began to work,

Wayne smiled at his daughter and said, "Wendy, this is Kyle Rogers."

Kyle's full attention was focused on the job at hand as he tried to disengage the fishing line without causing Wayne too much discomfort. He did stop long enough to mumble, "Nice to meet you."

"Are you going to be able to get that line off Dad without breaking it?" Wendy asked, glancing at Kyle.

"That's what we're trying to find out, Miss Campbell," Steve answered. "If you'll just move aside so we can have more room to —"

"My daughter's name is Wendy," Wayne interrupted.

"I'm really sorry about all this," Wendy said apologetically. "I'm sure you busy men have better things to do than untangle a fishing line."

"That's okay, Wendy," Kyle said kindly. "We were free when the call came in, and this could have been a real emergency. What if that line had gotten tangled around your dad's neck?"

Wendy nodded and waited silently as Kyle and his partner tried unsuccessfully to unwind the line. Finally, when their efforts seemed futile, Steve took out a pair of scissors from his belt pouch and began to cut.

After a few minutes Kyle announced, "There you go, Mr. Campbell. Freedom at last!"

Wayne smiled as the paramedics helped him to his feet and onto the couch.

"Are you planning a fishing trip in the near future, Mr. Campbell?" Kyle asked as he moved aside the fishing pole that was still leaning against the couch.

"No — no — not really," Wayne sputtered. "I mean, maybe —"

Wendy gave her dad a quizzical look, but when he didn't acknowledge her, she turned to face Kyle. "If you think Dad's okay, then I'll excuse myself to go fix us some lunch. I need to get back to the barbershop by one."

"You're a barber?" Kyle asked, raising his eyebrows. *Wow! This really is a day full of surprises.*

She nodded. "I have been for the last five years."

"Wendy and I used to be partners," Wayne put in. "Then my rheumatoid arthritis got the best of me, and I finally had to hang up my shaving gear and retire the old scissors." He grunted. "Now I'm just a worthless, crippled widower who sits around wishing he could do something worthwhile with his life."

Steve was already moving toward the door, but Kyle wasn't in any hurry to leave just yet. He pulled out a chair from the dining room table and placed it directly in front of Wayne. He took a seat and leaned forward. "Look, Mr. Campbell, none of God's children are worthless. Just because you're a bit hampered by your arthritis doesn't mean you can't do something worthwhile or have an active social life."

Wayne's eyes lit up. "You really think so?" He turned to Wendy. "Did you hear that? This nice young man thinks I have potential."

Wendy opened her mouth as if to

comment, but was cut off when Steve held up the medication box and asked, "You about ready to head out, Kyle?"

Kyle waved one hand toward the front door. "You can wait for me in the truck. I'll just be a few more minutes."

Steve shrugged, grabbed the rest of their medical cases, and headed out the door.

"You know, Mr. Campbell —" Kyle began.

"Wayne. Please call me Wayne."

Kyle smiled and pointed toward the Bible lying on the coffee table. "I see you have a copy of the Good Book over there."

When Wayne nodded, Kyle continued. "I hope that means you put your faith in God."

"I try to, but I don't get to church much these days."

"My father doesn't drive the car anymore," Wendy explained.

Kyle eyed her with speculation. "What about you? Don't you drive?"

"Of course I do." She frowned. "Why do you ask?"

Before Kyle could respond, Wayne cut right in. "I bought Wendy a new car for her twenty-fourth birthday last month, and she makes a great chauffeur."

"Dad!" Wendy exclaimed. "I don't think Mr. Rogers cares how old I am or that you just bought me a car."

Wayne shrugged and offered her an impish, teasing smile. "He did ask if you could drive."

Wendy drew in a deep breath and blew it out with such force, Kyle felt concern. "Are you all right, Miss Campbell?"

"I'm perfectly fine," she insisted. With a dimpled smile she added, "Thanks so much for rescuing Dad. I'm relieved there was no fishing hook involved and that it wasn't anything really serious. If you'll excuse me, I do need to fix lunch so I can get back to work."

Wendy started for the kitchen, but she stopped in her tracks when her father called, "Say, why don't we ask the paramedics to join us for lunch? You wouldn't mind fixing a little extra soup and some juicy roast beef sandwiches, would you, honey?"

Kyle glanced over at Wendy. She seemed a bit flustered, and he had a sudden desire to put her at ease. "I'm meeting someone for lunch, but thanks anyway," he said quickly.

Wendy's ears burned like a three-alarm fire. *What would possess Dad to invite someone for lunch without conferring with me first? It's just not like him to do something like that.* She shook her head, trying to make some sense out of this whole scene. One minute she had been frightened out of her wits by the sound of a siren, only to see the rescue truck stop in front of her house. The next moment, she was paralyzed with fear at the thought of her father being seriously hurt. Then she felt relief flood her soul when the paramedics were able to get Dad free and discovered that he hadn't been injured in any way by the fishing line. Now Dad was inviting strangers to lunch! What was going on here, anyway?

"You take care, Mr. Campbell, and remember — God loves you," Kyle said, breaking into Wendy's disconcerting thoughts. "I'm sure if you pray about it, you can find something worthwhile to do." He smiled at Wendy. "It was nice meeting you."

Wendy's heartbeat picked up slightly, but she merely nodded and closed the door behind Kyle Rogers.

"Didn't you think those guys were great? Especially Kyle. What a nice young man he seems to be," her father said.

Wendy shrugged her shoulders. Kyle was nice, all right. And good-looking, too. His dark, wavy hair looked like something she would enjoy cutting, and those eyes — the color of her favorite chocolate candy.

She shook her head, as if to knock some sense into it. She couldn't allow herself to think such thoughts. What had come over her, anyway?

"Paramedics are supposed to be good, Dad, or else they wouldn't be in the rescue business." Wendy flopped onto the couch. She grabbed a throw pillow and hugged it close to her chest. Her hands still trembled from the scare she'd just had, not to mention her unexplained attraction to one *very nice* paramedic. She felt a humdinger of a headache coming on, too. All thoughts of food suddenly faded.

"I know all about what paramedics are trained for," Dad said with a smile. "Allied Health Technical College in Grangely not only teaches emergency medical services but gives their students plenty of hands-on experience in the campus lab. The classroom training covers everything from cardiology basics to defensive driving of their emergency vehicles."

Wendy's mouth dropped open. "Just how in the world did you find out so much about paramedic training?" Before he could respond, she hurried on. "And why, Dad? Why would you need to know all that stuff?"

Dad smiled, causing his steel blue eyes to crinkle around the edges. "You know me. I'm always reading and doing some kind of research." He repositioned himself on the couch, then leaned his head against the cushions. "What else is there for a poor old cripple to do all day?"

Wendy shook her head. "You're

only fifty, Dad. That's not old. And, while you're not filthy rich, you certainly aren't poor either. I make an adequate living at the barbershop, and your disability benefits help quite a bit."

He pointed a knobby finger at her. "You didn't bother touching on the subject of me being a cripple though, did you? That's because it's true."

Wendy began to knead her forehead. "Listen, Dad, I know being housebound so much of the time is probably getting to you, but you can't start feeling sorry for yourself. It won't solve a thing."

"Who says I'm feeling sorry for myself?" he snapped.

"Dad, I apologize."

"No, I'm the one who needs to do that," he said in a more subdued tone. "I don't know what came over me. I shouldn't have barked at you." He frowned and reached down to massage one leg. "Guess I'm in a bit of pain right now. It's making me kind of touchy and out of sorts."

Wendy was immediately on her feet. "Oh Dad, I'm so sorry! How thoughtless of me to forget about the aspirin you usually take with your meal." She started toward the kitchen but turned back. "Listen, about lunch —"

"Just a bowl of soup will be fine for me," he interrupted. "Forget about the roast beef sandwich. I'm not all that hungry anyway."

She shook her head. "No, I wasn't going to ask that."

"What then?"

"I was wondering why you invited

those paramedics to stay for lunch."

"They looked hungry," he replied with a Cheshire cat grin.

"Yeah, right," she countered. "You're such a kidder, Dad."

"I just thought it would be nice if we had some company for a change," Dad said, giving her a look that resembled a little-boy pout.

Wendy came back to kneel in front of the couch. "Dad, if you're really that bored, why not invite Fred or even good old Clyde over for lunch one of these days? If you give me some advance notice, I might even be willing to whip up something really nice."

He scowled. "Fred and Clyde? You've gotta be kidding, Wendy. Why, those guys and their same old jokes are boring."

"Dad!"

He smiled sheepishly. "Well, maybe not boring exactly, but certainly not full of vim and vigor, like those nice paramedics seemed to be."

Wendy groaned inwardly. She just didn't understand what had come over Dad. Maybe he was in his second childhood or something. Maybe he thought he needed to be around younger people in order to feel youthful.

She gave him a weak smile. "I *am* going out to the kitchen now. I think a bowl of chicken noodle soup might help both of our moods."

CHAPTER 3

"Oh brother," Wendy fumed as she closed the door behind what she hoped would be her last Friday morning customer. She needed at least half an hour to repair the damage left in the wake of little Jeffrey Peterson. Maybe by the time she'd eaten and checked on Dad, her emotions would have settled down.

"If the rest of my day goes as badly as the last few hours, I may consider closing this shop and finding a *normal* job!" she said, leaning against the edge of the counter.

First thing this morning, the Miller brothers came in — without appointments, of course. Rufus and Alvin lived in an old shack just outside of town, and the mere sight of the tall, gangly men made Wendy's stomach churn. Their clothes were always grimy and smelled like week-old dirty socks. The brothers' greasy, matted hair looked as if it hadn't been washed since their last cut, nearly eight weeks ago. It was a wonder they didn't have a head full of lice!

If that wasn't bad enough, both of the men sported the foulest breath she'd ever had the misfortune of smelling. To add insult to injury, Alvin spit his chewing tobacco into the potted palm sitting in one corner of the barbershop.

Jeffrey Peterson had been her next

client, and what a time she'd had trying to get the active three-year-old to sit still! Even with the aide of the booster seat, he'd sat much too low. It was a miracle Wendy didn't take off an ear instead of the unruly mass of bright red hair, glued together by a hunk of bubble gum that could only be cut out. To make matters worse, Jeffrey managed to leave another wad of sticky gum on the arm of her barber's chair.

"Now wouldn't that give someone a nice bonus when they sit down, expecting a haircut or shave?" Wendy grumbled, scrubbing the gummy clump and wondering about the logic of buying that antique, claw-foot gum ball machine. "Maybe I should have gone to beauty school like my friend Sharon."

Suddenly the bell above her shop door rang, indicating another customer.

She looked up from her gum-removal project and scowled. It was Gabe Hunter, the very man old Clyde Baxter wanted to link her up with. *That will never happen,* Wendy fumed. *Gabe acts like a conceited creep, and the guy thinks he's every woman's dream come true.*

A quick glance at the wall clock told her it was eleven thirty. While she certainly wasn't thrilled about this particular customer, she knew she could manage to squeeze in one more haircut before lunch.

"Morning, Wendy," Gabe said with a wink. "You're lookin' as pert and pretty as always."

"Flattery will get you nowhere,

Gabe," Wendy said through clenched teeth. "At least not with me."

Gabe removed his leather jacket and carelessly threw it over one of the old opera-style seats in the small waiting room. "Aw, come on. You know you find me irresistible. I mean, how could you not? I'm probably your best-looking customer, not to mention the fact that I'm a great tipper." Gabe plopped into the chair Wendy had been scrubbing and planted his hairy hand inches from hers.

"Why don't you sit in that chair?" she suggested, pulling her hand away and motioning to what used to be her father's barber chair. "As you can probably see, this one has recently been initiated."

Gabe shrugged and moved to the

other chair. "You know what?"

"No, what?" Wendy shot back.

"I don't have to start work until two today. How about you and me going over to Pete's Place and sharin' a large pepperoni pizza?"

"I'm working."

"Well, you've gotta take a lunch break, right?" he persisted.

Moving away from the gummed-up chair, Wendy grabbed a clean cotton drape and hooked it around Gabe's humongous neck. He'd been a star football player during high school, and now he worked as a mechanic for the only car repair shop in Plumers. Every time the brute came in for a haircut, he tried to come on to Wendy. Some of the town's young single women might be fooled by his good looks and somewhat crass charisma, but not Wendy. She'd been burned once, and she couldn't let it happen again. Especially not with some six-foot-two, blue-eyed charmer who didn't have the good sense to know when to keep his mouth shut.

"Well, how about it?"

"How about what?" Wendy side-stepped.

"Lunch — with me." He gave her another wink.

"I'm going home for lunch so I can check on Dad," she said evenly.

Gabe threw both hands in the hair, nearly pulling the cotton drape off his neck. "Whatever!"

"How much do you want off?" Wendy ignored his childish antics and made a firm attempt to get down to business. If she didn't get this guy out of the chair soon, not only would she be late for lunch, but what was left of her sanity would probably be long gone as well.

"Same as usual," came the casual reply. Then Gabe added with a wide grin, "You sure do have pretty blue eyes, Wendy Campbell."

Wendy closed those pretty eyes briefly and offered up a pleading entreaty. *Oh Lord, please give me strength.* It wasn't really much of a prayer, but it was the first one she'd petitioned God for since her father's 911 scare three days ago.

Wendy had accepted Christ as her Savior at an early age. She'd attended Sunday school and church for many years, too. Prayer and Bible reading used to be an important part of her life.

It wasn't until she began dating

Dale Carlson while she was attending Bailey's Barber School in Spokane that things started to change. Dale had been the perfect Christian . . . or so he'd let on. Dale's mask of self-righteousness came catapulting off when he began making unwanted advances, asking Wendy to sacrifice her chastity. Not more than a week after putting Dale in his place, Wendy discovered he'd been seeing Michelle Stiles the whole time while coming on to her. The entire episode had shaken her faith in men and her own good judgment. Her relationship with Christ had suffered, as she was no longer sure she could even trust God.

"I don't think you're gonna get much hair taken off by just standin' there frowning like the world is about to end," Gabe declared, disrupting Wendy's reflections.

She shook her head, trying to re-establish her thoughts and get down to the business at hand. The sooner she got garish Gabe's curly black hair trimmed, the better it would be for both of them.

Half an hour later, Wendy had just taken the clippers to Gabe's neck and was about to dust him off when he announced, "That's not quite how I want it. Could you take a little more off the sides?"

Exasperated with this big hulk of a man, Wendy gritted her teeth, forcing herself as always to comply with the customer's wishes.

"I wouldn't mind having one of those neck rubs you're so famous for," Gabe said when the haircut was finished. "Yep, it sure would feel great to have your soft hands work some of the kinks out of my neck."

Right here is where I draw the line with this guy, Wendy reasoned silently. "I just don't have time for that today, Gabe," she said through tight lips. "I barely managed to squeeze you in for a haircut."

"You're sure not very sociable." Gabe stepped down from the chair. "I've spent the last half hour telling you how great we'd be together, and all you've done is give me the silent treatment."

Wendy chewed on her bottom lip, trying to hold back the words that threatened to roll off her tongue. She moved toward the cash register, hoping he would follow.

He did, but as soon as he handed

her the money, Gabe blurted out, "If your mood doesn't improve some, you might start to lose customers." He shrugged into his black leather jacket. "Seriously, most folks don't come in here for just a shave or a good haircut, you know."

Wendy eyed him speculatively. "Oh? Why *do* they come in, Gabe?"

"A barber is kind of like a bartender," he said with another one of his irritating winks.

"Is that so?" Wendy could feel her temperature begin to rise, so she took a few deep breaths to keep from saying the wrong thing.

"Yep," Gabe retaliated. "Many barbershops — especially ones that operate in small towns like Plumers — are noted as places where folks can share their problems, tell a few jokes, and let their hair down." He draped his muscular arm across her slender shoulders and smirked. "Get it, unfriendly Wendy? A good barber is supposed to be *friendly* and courteous to their customers."

Wendy grimaced. Gabe had stepped on her toes with that statement. She really did try to be polite to her customers, no matter how much they might irritate her. With Gabe, it was different. She didn't need men like him trying to put her down or take advantage. And she certainly wasn't going to give him the chance to make a complete fool of her the way Dale had.

"Have a nice day, Gabe," Wendy said in a strained voice.

He nodded curtly. "Sure. You, too."

The door was closing behind Gabe

when Wendy heard it — that ear-piercing whine of a siren. She shuddered and glanced out the window. An emergency vehicle sped past the shop and headed up her street.

"Oh no," she moaned, "not again. Please, God, don't let it be going to my house this time."

Kyle Rogers couldn't believe he was being called back to the same house he'd been to only a few days ago. The dispatcher said Wayne had called asking for help because he was in terrible pain. What really seemed strange was the fact that the 911 call had come in about the same time as three days earlier. He shrugged. *Probably just a coincidence.*

"Ready?" Kyle asked Steve, opening the door of their truck and grabbing his rescue case.

"Ready," Steve said with a nod.

Kyle rapped on the front door. A distressed-sounding voice called out, "It's open. Come in."

When they stepped into the living room, they found Wayne lying on the couch.

"What is it, sir?" Kyle asked, kneeling on the floor in front of the couch. He had just put on his gloves when Wayne reached out to clasp his hand.

"I–I've got a cramp in my leg, and it's killing me! Wendy's not home from work yet, but she should be here soon." He drew his leg up and winced in pain as Kyle began probing.

"Is this where the cramp is, Mr. Campbell?"

Wayne shook his head. "No. I mean, yes — I think it's there."

"Do you get leg cramps very often?" Kyle inquired.

"Sometimes. It goes along with having rheumatoid arthritis, you know." Wayne glanced at the door. "Where is Wendy, anyway? She should be home by now."

Kyle gently massaged Wayne's contorted limb. "Is this helping any?"

Wayne thrashed about. "No, no, it still hurts like crazy. I think it's getting worse, not better!" He began moaning, then started gasping for breath. "I can't take it! I can't take any more!"

"Calm down, Mr. Campbell," Steve admonished. "You're only making it worse."

"He's hyperventilating, Steve. Get a bag."

Steve reached into their supply case

and quickly followed instructions, placing a brown paper sack over Wayne's nose and mouth. "Do you think he could be having a panic attack, Kyle?"

Kyle nodded. "It looks that way. Once he begins to relax, we can work on that leg cramp."

The uncooperative patient pushed the bag aside. "Wendy — she —"

"I don't think we should be concerned about your daughter right now," Kyle asserted. "Let's get you calmed down; then we'll see if we can't take care of that charley horse." Kyle took the paper sack from Wayne and held it to his face again. "Breathe as normally as you can, and please, no more talking until we say."

A red-faced Wayne finally complied,

settling back against the throw pillows.

Steve had just started to massage the leg again when Wendy came flying into the house.

"What happened? Is my dad sick? He wasn't playing with his fishing line again, I hope." Her eyes were huge as saucers, and her face white like chalk.

Kyle eyed her with concern. "Steady now, Miss Campbell. Why don't you have a seat?"

With an audible moan, Wendy dropped into the rocking chair. "Please tell me what's wrong with Dad."

"He called 911 because he was in terrible pain. When we got here, he said his leg had cramped up," Kyle explained.

"What's the paper sack for?"

"He started hyperventilating," Kyle replied.

"What would cause that?" She leaned forward with both hands on her knees.

"Probably a panic attack, brought on by the stress of not being able to get the pain stopped," Steve interjected.

Wayne was trying to remove the sack again, but Kyle shook his head. "Let's keep it there for a few more moments, Mr. Campbell. It will help you calm down; then you'll be able to breathe better." Kyle turned to Wendy. "Does your father get many severe leg cramps?"

She shrugged. "Some, but nothing he can't usually work out with a bit of massage or some heat." She looked at her father with obvious concern. "Dad, when did the cramping start, and why didn't you call me instead of 911?"

Kyle pulled the sack away so Wayne could respond to his daughter's question.

"I didn't want to bother you," Wayne mumbled.

"Wouldn't it have been better to interrupt my day than to make these men answer a call that could have been handled with a simple heating pad?"

Wayne tipped his head to one side and blinked rapidly. "Guess I didn't think about that. I just wanted to get some relief, and it hurt like crazy, so —"

"When was the last time you had some aspirin?" Steve asked.

"He has to take it with food, or it upsets his stomach," Wendy glanced over at her Dad with an anxious look. "I'd better fix some lunch so you can take your pills."

Wayne nodded and pulled himself to a sitting position. "The leg cramp's gone now." He looked up at Wendy. "Some of that take-and-bake pizza you bought last night would sure be good."

"Okay, Dad, if that's what you want."

Wendy was almost to the kitchen when Wayne called, "Let's invite these nice young men to join us. How about it, guys? It's lunchtime. Does pizza sound good to you?"

"Sure does," Steve was quick to say.

"Count me in, too," Kyle agreed. He cast a quick glance at Wendy.

"That is, if it's not too much trouble."

Wendy smiled. "No trouble at all."

Wendy sat across the table from her dad, watching with interest as he and the other two men interacted. *He really is lonesome,* she thought ruefully. *How could I have let this happen?* She began to massage her forehead. *I've got to figure out some way to help fill Dad's lonely hours.*

"Wendy, are you listening? Kyle asked you a question."

Wendy snapped to attention at the sound of Dad's deep voice. "What was it?" She looked at Kyle, who sat in the chair beside her.

"I was wondering about your barbershop."

"What about it?"

"What are your hours? Do you only take appointments?"

"I do take walk-ins, but many of my customers make appointments. The barbershop is open Tuesday through Saturday, from nine in the morning until five at night, with an hour off for lunch at noon." Wendy eyed him curiously. "Why do you ask?" Her heart fluttered as she awaited his answer. Was she actually hoping he might come in for a haircut?

Kyle shrugged. "Just wondering."

"How did you become a barber?" Steve asked. "Isn't that kind of unusual work for a woman?"

"Actually, I've heard that some of the finest barbers are women," Kyle inserted before Wendy could answer.

"That's right," agreed her father, "and my Wendy girl is one of them.

Why, she graduated in the top five of her barbering class."

"Spoken like a proud papa," Kyle said with a grin.

"Dad tends to be a little bit prejudiced," Wendy was quick to say. "After all, I am his only daughter."

"And the only breadwinner these days," Dad added, bringing a note of regret into the conversation.

"I served my apprenticeship under Dad," Wendy said, hoping to dispel the gloomy look on Dad's face. "He sometimes forgets that I wasn't always so capable." She shook her head. "If you had time to listen, I'll bet he could tell you some real horror stories about how I messed up several people's hair during those early years. Dad is a wonderful, ever-patient teacher, and if I do anything well, I owe it all to him."

Steve laughed, but Kyle seemed to be deep in thought. Finally, he reached for another slice of pizza and took a bite. "Mmm . . . this is sure good." He washed it down with a gulp of iced tea, then changed the subject. "Say, Mr. Campbell, I know you were tying some flies the other day, and I was just wondering if you've done much fishing lately. I hear there's some pretty good trout in several of the streams around here."

Dad rubbed his chin thoughtfully. "I used to fish a lot — back when I could still function on my own, that is."

"When was the last time you went fishing?" Kyle asked, leaning forward on his elbows.

"Well, let's see now," Dad began. "I guess it's been a little more than two years since my last fishing trip. My buddy Fred and I went up to Plumers Creek one spring morning. We sat on the grassy banks all day, just basking in the warm sun, shootin' the breeze, and reeling in some of the most gorgeous trout you'd ever want to see."

"Plumers Creek is a great place to fish," Steve put in. "I've been there a few times myself. How come you've never been back, sir?"

"I don't really think Dad's up to any fishing trips," Wendy interjected. "You saw the way his leg cramped up." She grimaced. "I'm sorry, but there are times when I have to wonder if all men ever think about is hunting, fishing, and telling contemptible jokes."

Three pairs of eyes focused on Wendy, and Dad's face had turned as red as the pizza sauce.

"I, uh, think maybe we'd better go," Steve said, sliding his chair away from the table. "The pizza was great. Thanks, Miss Campbell."

"No, no, you can't leave yet!" Dad protested. "I mean, we were just beginning to get acquainted."

"Our lunch hour's not quite over yet, so we can hang out a few more minutes," Kyle said.

"I really do need to get back to work, Dad." Wendy stood up and grabbed the empty pizza pan. Not only was she going to be late for work if she didn't leave now, but she didn't care much for the direction this conversation was going. There was no point giving Dad false hope, and besides, sitting next to ever-smiling Kyle Rogers was making her nervous.

"Since your cramp is gone and you seem to be feeling better," Wendy said, moving across the room, "I'll leave you in the capable hands of these paramedics."

CHAPTER 4

Twice in one week! Wendy fretted. *Was it a coincidence that Dad called 911 so often, or did he really think it was an emergency? Was Dad merely "crying wolf" just to get some special attention?*

Wendy was glad they'd made it through the weekend without any more problems. Yesterday she scheduled a doctor's appointment for her dad; today, right after work, she'd be taking him in for an exam. He didn't know she'd done it though. He'd been so adamant about his leg feeling better and had assured her several times that there was no more cramping and no need to see Dr. Hastings until his regular checkup later in the month. She'd tell him about his appointment and try to make him see reason when she went home for lunch today.

Wendy's nerves felt all tied up in knots. Maybe that was why she'd been so testy the other day when the paramedics were talking to Dad about fishing. She didn't need any more chilling 911 calls to deal with either. What she really needed was a little peace and quiet. Maybe she should close the shop for a few days and stay home with Dad.

"That's probably not the best solution though," she murmured as she put the OPEN sign in the front door of the barbershop. "What I really need is to concentrate on finding some way to make him feel more useful and less lonely. If Dad won't take the initiative, then maybe *I* should give some of his buddies a call about lunch."

Wendy's first scheduled appointment wasn't until ten o'clock, so that gave her a whole hour. She drew in a deep breath and reached for the telephone.

After several rings, a gravelly voice came on the line. "Fred Hastings here. What can I do ya for?"

"Fred, this is Wendy Campbell, and I need to ask you a favor."

"Sure, ask away," Fred said with a deep chuckle.

"You and Dad are pretty good friends. Isn't that right?" Wendy drummed her fingers against the counter where the old rotary-dial phone sat.

"Yep. Right as rain. Why do ya ask?"

"When was the last time you paid Dad a visit?"

There was a long pause.

"Fred? Are you still there?"

"Yep, I'm still here. Let's see now . . . I think it was last month, when I dropped some fishin' magazines by your house."

Wendy grimaced. Fishing magazines? Those were the last things Dad needed, since he could no longer fish. What was the point of adding fuel to the fire by reminding him of what he couldn't do? No wonder he was trying to tie fishing flies.

"Your dad and me went fishin' a few years ago, and —"

A low moan escaped Wendy's lips as Fred began a long, detailed narration of the last time he and her dad had gone up to Plumers Creek. She was trying to figure out the best way to politely get back to the reason for her call when the front door opened, jingling the bell and announcing an unscheduled customer. Wendy turned her head toward the door, and her mouth fell open. There stood Kyle Rogers, wearing a pair of blue jeans and a red flannel shirt. He looked so manly and rugged. Kind of like one of those lumberjacks who often came into the shop — only he was much better-looking. Another distinction was the fact that none of the woodsmen wore a religious pin on their shirt pocket, announcing to the world that they were trying to live and respond to others as Jesus would.

What would Jesus do right now? Wendy mused. She forced her thoughts back to the one-way phone conversation and cleared her throat loudly. "Um, Fred — someone just came into the shop. I'll have to call you back another time." She hung up and slowly moved toward Kyle.

He smiled softly and ran long fingers through his thick brown hair. "Hi, Wendy. Do you have time to squeeze me in?"

"Squeeze you in?" she squeaked.

"For a shave and a haircut." Kyle rubbed his stubbly chin and chuckled. "I've heard through the grapevine that you not only cut hair well but can give a really close shave."

Was Kyle flirting with her? Well, why wouldn't he be? Gabe did, and a few other guys seemed to think they could make a play for the town's lady barber, too. Why should Paramedic Rogers be any different? "I was trying to get some phone calls made, but I guess I could manage a shave and haircut," she said as politely as possible.

He started to move toward her, then stopped. "If this is going to be a problem, I could make an appointment and come back a little later. This is my day off, so —"

Wendy held up one hand. "No, that's okay. The rest of my day is pretty full, so it'll have to be now, I guess."

"Okay, thanks," Kyle said with a grin. "If I wait much longer for a haircut, I might get fired for looking like a bum."

Wendy reached for a cotton drape cloth and snapped it open, nodding toward her barber chair. "Have a seat."

Kyle quickly complied. When he was seated, with his head leaning against the headrest, Wendy hit the lever on the side of the chair, tipping it back so she could begin the shave.

"I'm sorry about the other day," Kyle said while she slapped a big glob of slick white shaving foam against one side of his face.

"Oh? What do you have to be sorry about?" she asked, keeping her tone strictly businesslike.

"For upsetting you." Kyle turned his head slightly so she could lather the other side as well. "You were upset when we started talking about fishing, right?"

Wendy shrugged. "Not upset, really. I just don't like it when someone gives Dad false hope."

"False hope? Oh, you mean about going fishing?"

Wendy nodded curtly. "You'd better close your mouth now, or you might end up with it full of shaving cream."

Kyle could only nod at this point, because she'd just placed a pleasantly hot, wet towel over his entire face. He drew in a deep breath, closed his eyes, and allowed himself to relax. Wow! This felt like heaven. Too bad the cute little blond administering all this special attention didn't seem to care much for him. She seemed distant, and if his instincts were working as well as usual, Kyle guessed her father might be right. Maybe Wendy did feel strapped, having to care for him and run a barbershop by herself. He couldn't even begin to imagine what it must be like for her to give shaves and cut men's hair five days a week. From what he'd witnessed in other barbershops, some of the clientele could be pretty crass and rude at times.

Kyle's forehead wrinkled. *I wonder if either Wendy or Wayne ever does anything just for fun. Maybe what they need is something positive to focus on. With God's help, maybe I can figure out some way to help them both.*

Wendy let Kyle sit with the warm towel on his face for several minutes, knowing that the procedure would not only cleanse the face, but also soften his bristly whiskers. When she lifted it off, he opened his mouth as if he had to say something, but she quickly wiped his face clean and applied more shaving cream.

"Phase two," she explained at his questioning look.

He nodded.

Wendy began to use the straight razor on her client's appealing face. She'd shaved a lot of handsome faces during her years as a barber, but none had ever evoked quite the response from her as Kyle Rogers. It was unnerving the way he looked at her — with dark, serious eyes and a smile that actually seemed sincere.

That's just it, Wendy groaned inwardly. *He "seems" sincere . . . but is he really? Probably not,* she silently acknowledged. *Except for Dad, I can't think of a single man who is truly sincere.* She drew in a deep breath, bringing all the pain of the past right along with it. *Dale wasn't sincere, that's for sure.*

"Are you okay?"

She blinked. "Huh? What do you mean?"

"You look like you're distressed about something."

Wendy gave her head a slight toss. "Sure, I'm fine." She hit the lever on the side of the chair, and it shot into a sitting position with such force, Kyle's head snapped forward. "Oh! I'm sorry about that," she said, reaching for a bottle of aftershave lotion on the shelf behind her. "This chair's a genuine antique, and sometimes when the levers are messed with, it seems to have a mind of its own."

Wendy patted the spicy liquid onto Kyle's freshly shaven face. He winced. "Do all your customers receive such treatment, or do you only reserve the rough stuff for guys like me?"

"Sorry," she said again. "Maybe your face is more sensitive than some."

"Guess so. That's what happens when you rely on an electric instead of a razor blade." He smiled up at her. "You sure have pretty blue eyes, do you know that?"

Oh no . . . here it comes, she fumed. *That lay-it-on-thick, make-a-move-on-Wendy routine.* She should have guessed Kyle was too good to be true. "How much hair do you want cut off?" she asked evenly.

He shook his wavy, dark mane.

"Guess maybe you'd better take about an inch all the way around."

Wendy deftly began snipping here and there, never taking her eyes off the job at hand, trying to still the racing of her heart. Was she really dumb enough to be attracted to Kyle Rogers, or was her heart beating a staccato because she was irritated about his slick-talking ways and the silly, crooked grin he kept casting in her direction?

"Did you drive your dad to church on Sunday?" Kyle asked unexpectedly.

"No, I didn't. Why do you ask?"

"When I responded to Wayne's first 911 call, he made some mention of not getting out much," Kyle reminded her. "He said he can't drive to church anymore, so I was thinking maybe I could —"

"Well, don't worry about it," Wendy asserted. "If Dad wants a ride, he knows all he has to do is ask me."

"Do you go out much?"

"Huh?" Just where was this conversation leading? She stopped her work and turned his chair so she could see both of their reflections in the antique beveled mirror. "Just so you know — I don't date — period."

He frowned. "Really? In your line of work, I thought you'd probably have a bunch of guys standing in line."

"I'm far too busy trying to keep this shop running," she said. "And as I'm sure you must have noticed, Dad needs my help at home."

"I realize that, Wendy, but you do have a life of your own, and —"

"No, actually, I don't!" She gave the chair a sharp turn so she could resume work.

"Then I suppose you wouldn't be interested in attending a Christian concert at my church in Grangely tonight?" Kyle asked.

Wendy clenched her jaw so hard she could feel a dull ache. Never had she wanted to finish a haircut so badly. What was it about Kyle that affected her so?

"I plan to spend the evening playing a few games with my dad," she informed him. "I think he's bored and needs me to spend more quality time with him."

"Maybe he needs to get out of the house more," Kyle suggested.

Wendy stopped cutting again and held the scissors directly over her client's head. "I appreciate your concerns, Kyle, but my father's needs are really *my* business."

He shrugged. "I just thought Wayne might like to go to that concert with us, that's all. There's a very special widow who goes to my church, and since your dad said he likes to fish —"

"Fish?" She grimaced. "What's fishing got to do with a church concert?"

"Nothing," he admitted. "Maybe everything."

Wendy started cutting his hair again. "I don't follow you."

"Edna Stone — the widow I just mentioned — likes to fish," Kyle explained. "In fact, she goes fishing nearly every week. If we could get your dad and Edna to meet, they might strike up a friendship and maybe even go fishing together."

So it really wasn't a date he was asking her on after all. It was her dad he was trying to help. Wendy had obviously misjudged his intentions. However, that reality didn't make her feel much better. In fact, she wasn't sure how she was feeling about now.

"So what are you?" she asked. "Some kind of 911 matchmaker?" Before Kyle could respond, she rushed on. "Really, the last thing Dad needs is some fisherwoman." She made a few more scissor snips, then added, "And need I remind you that he is disabled?"

"I know that, Wendy, but it doesn't mean he has to stop living."

"He's gotten along just fine for the last ten years without a wife, and I don't think he needs or even wants one now."

Kyle held up one hand. "I wasn't insinuating that Wayne and Edna would soon be walking down the aisle together." He grinned. "Of course, I suppose that could happen if the two of them should hit it off."

Wendy placed her scissors on the counter, then stepped in front of the barber chair. "I'm only going to say this once, and I hope you under-stand."

Kyle nodded. "I'm all ears."

Wendy blinked back threatening tears that had unexpectedly filled her eyes. "Dad doesn't need a woman friend or a wife. He just needs me to help fill his lonely hours." She inhaled sharply. "And I'm already working on that."

CHAPTER 5

As Kyle closed the door of his Bronco and started up the engine, he fought the urge to go back to Campbell's Barbershop. He dropped his head forward until it rested on the steering wheel. *Am I treading on thin ice, Lord?* he prayed. *Am I interested in Wayne and Wendy Campbell because I see a real need, or am I merely experiencing some kind of unexplained physical attraction to the cute little blond barber?*

Kyle didn't date much, mostly because of his crazy work schedule. However, if he were completely honest, he'd have to admit that he was concerned about establishing any kind of serious relationship that might lead to marriage. The life of a paramedic was far from ideal, and trying to balance his career with a wife and children would be difficult at best. He had no right to subject another human being to his "calling." He really should only date women he would never be apt to become romantically involved with.

"Wendy's father says he's a Christian, but I'm not so sure about Wendy," Kyle said, lifting his head from the steering wheel and turning the key in the ignition. She'd made no profession of Christianity and apparently didn't attend church. "She doesn't seem to have any interest in men or dating either," he murmured.

He pulled away from the curb with a slight smile tugging at the corners of his mouth. "Wayne Campbell needs some help, and I'm pretty sure Wendy does, too, Lord. So if I am the one to help them, I'm asking for Your guidance in all this."

Wendy was closing the barbershop at noon when she heard the distinctive whine of sirens in the distance. As the sound drew closer, she felt a funny feeling in the pit of her stomach. She uttered a quick prayer. "Not again, Lord. Please don't let it be another false alarm."

Wendy grabbed her coat. "What am I saying? Do I want a real emergency this time?"

She jerked the door open just in time to see the rescue vehicle fly past her shop. Stepping onto the sidewalk, Wendy could see clear up the street. She watched in horror as the truck came to a full stop in front of her house.

"Oh no!" she groaned. Not sure whether to be angry with her father or concerned for his welfare, Wendy made a mad dash for home. She stepped onto the porch just in time to meet Steve and an older paramedic who identified himself as Phil Givens. "What's the problem?" she asked breathlessly.

Steve shook his head. "Not sure. When we received the call, the 911 operator said she could hardly make heads or tails out of the man's frantic plea for help."

This had better be for real this time, Wendy fussed inwardly. But even as the words flew into her mind, she reprimanded herself. If Dad really was sick, he needed help, and she needed to be with him. She threw open the front door and spotted her father, sitting in his recliner. He didn't look one bit sick. In fact, Wendy thought he looked more anxious than ill.

"Where's Kyle?" her father asked, looking past Wendy and the two rescue men who had followed her inside.

"Kyle has the day off, Mr. Campbell," Steve explained. "Phil always fills in for him on Tuesdays."

Before Dad could say anything more, both men had opened their rescue cases and donned their surgical gloves.

"What seems to be the problem?"

Phil asked in a businesslike tone. "I understand your call was pretty vague."

"I — uh — was feeling kind of dizzy," he stammered. "I'm much better now though. Probably just got up too quickly."

"We're here, so we may as well check you out," Phil said with a curt nod.

"I agree," Steve put in. "It could be something serious this time."

Phil gave him an odd look. "What do you mean, *this* time?"

Steve shrugged. "This is the third call to this house in two weeks."

"And I just can't believe it," Wendy moaned. "What's the problem, Dad?"

He hung his head. "Nothing. I mean, I thought I was feeling kind of dizzy before, but now —"

"And now you're feeling just fine and dandy? Is that it?" Wendy lamented. She dropped to her knees in front of his chair. "Dad, do you know how bad you scared me?"

"We'll check him over in case there is something really wrong," Steve said before Dad could make any kind of reply.

Wendy turned to face the paramedic. "Just so you know, I have no pizza today."

Phil's expression revealed his obvious bewilderment. "Pizza? What's that supposed to mean?"

"Nothing. It doesn't mean anything at all," Dad cut in.

"Maybe what you need is a cat, Dad," Wendy muttered.

Dad looked at her as if she'd completely lost her mind. "I think you men had better go now," he mumbled. "My daughter and I have a few things to discuss."

Steve hesitated. "But you said you were feeling dizzy. Are you sure you're all right?"

"I'm fine, really." Dad struggled to sit up again. "Sorry about the wasted trip to Plumers."

"You really should think twice about calling 911," Phil said firmly. "We are extremely busy, and responding to unnecessary calls doesn't set very well with me."

Wendy gave the man an icy stare. "Dad *thought* he was sick."

Phil shot her a look of irritation in return, then nodded to Steve. "Let's get going."

"A cat or dog might not be such a bad idea," Steve whispered as Wendy saw them out the door.

"It's either that, or I may have to consider moving Dad to the Grangely Fire and Rescue Station," Wendy said with a faint smile. She closed the door and leaned heavily against it, wondering what she was going to say to Dad, and how to say it without hurting his feelings.

"Look, Dad," she began, moving back to the living room, "I know you're probably lonely, and —"

He held up one hand as if to silence her. "I'm afraid I have an admission to make."

"Oh, and what might that be?" she asked with raised eyebrows.

"All three of my 911 calls were trumped up."

Wendy waved both hands in the air. "No? You think?"

He laughed lightly, but she didn't respond to his mirth. Those calls had frightened her, and she saw nothing funny about calling out the paramedics for false alarms either.

He motioned her to take a seat. "It's like this, honey — I thought Kyle Rogers would be working today, so —"

"Kyle has the day off," Wendy interrupted. "He came into the barbershop for a shave and a haircut this morning."

Dad's face brightened considerably. "He did?"

Wendy nodded. "Yes, but it might be the first and last cut he ever gets at Campbell's Barbershop."

"Oh, Wendy! You didn't scare him off, I hope."

"Scare him off? What's that supposed to mean, Dad?"

"Kyle's a nice young Christian man, and I think he would make good husband material."

Wendy moaned. "Husband material? Oh, Dad, please don't tell me you've been trying to set us up."

He shrugged, a smile playing at the corners of his mouth. "Okay, I won't tell you that."

"Dad! How could you?"

He hung his head sheepishly. "I thought you needed a man. I thought it might help —"

The rest of his sentence was lost on Wendy. All she could think of was the fact that everything had finally come into crystal-clear focus. Dad wasn't really that lonely after all. The old schemer was trying to set her up. What in the world was she going to do about this?

Right after lunch, Wendy convinced her dad to take a nap. He had seemed a bit overwrought ever since the paramedics left, and she thought he needed some rest. Besides, it would give her a chance to think things through more clearly.

Wendy closed the door to his bedroom and headed across the hall to her own room. She grabbed the telephone from the small table by her bed and dialed the Grangely Clinic. Since Dad was feeling fine, she saw no reason for him to see Dr. Hastings this afternoon after all.

A few minutes later, the appointment she'd scheduled had been canceled, and Wendy hung up the receiver. At least, she thought it was hung up. Preoccupied with thoughts of Kyle, Dad, and her own self-doubts, Wendy missed fitting the receiver completely into the cradle. She left the room quickly and took a peek at Dad. He was sleeping like a baby, so she grabbed her coat and headed out the front door.

Outside the house, the air felt frigid. From the gray clouds gathering in the sky, it looked like it might even snow. Wendy stuffed her hands inside her pockets and hurried down the street toward her barbershop, hoping the storm wouldn't be too severe.

When she arrived at the shop, good old, joke-telling Clyde Baxter was waiting outside the door. He was leaning up against the building, just under the swirling, traditional candy-cane-style barber pole, blowing on his hands and stomping his feet up and down. "You're late," he grumbled, "and it's gettin' mighty cold out here. My eyes are sure smartin', too."

When Wendy apologized, his irritation seemed to vanish as quickly as it had come. He chuckled softly and said, "Say, here's a question for you, little lady. When are eyes not eyes?"

Wendy shrugged and opened the shop door. "Beats me."

"When the wind makes them water!" Clyde howled as he stepped inside, then slipped out of his heavy jacket and hung it on a wall peg.

Hanging up her own coat, Wendy let out a pathetic groan. "Sorry, Clyde, but I'm afraid I'm not in much of a laughing mood today. Things got a little confusing at home during lunch, and I ended up staying longer than usual."

"Everything okay with your dad?"

Wendy nodded. "Besides his arthritis, the only thing wrong with Dad is a very bad case of meddleitis."

Clyde's bushy white eyebrows shot up. "What's that supposed to mean?"

She shrugged. "Never mind. You probably wouldn't understand anyway."

"Try me," Clyde said as he took a seat in Wendy's chair and leaned his head back in readiness for a shave.

Wendy drew in a deep breath and let it out in a rush. "For some reason, Dad thinks I need a man, and he's been making 911 calls in order to play matchmaker." She grabbed a handful of shaving cream and was about to apply it to Clyde's face when he stopped her.

"Whoa, hold on just a minute, little lady. I wholeheartedly agree with the part about your needin' a man, but what's all this about Wayne calling 911?"

Wendy bit her bottom lip so hard she tasted blood. Wincing, she replied, "In the past two weeks, he's called the Grangely Fire and Rescue Department three times, and they were all false alarms."

"Are you sure? I mean, maybe his arthritis is gettin' the best of him, and he just can't cut the mustard no more," Clyde defended.

Wendy shook her head, patting the shaving foam into place on the old man's weathered cheeks. "They were *planned* false alarms, believe me."

Clyde squinted. "Even if they were,

what's that got to do with Wayne becomin' a matchmaker?"

"He's trying to pair me up with one of the paramedics who's been responding to his fake calls," Wendy replied. "It took awhile to learn the truth, but now that I know just what Dad's little game is, I've got a few games up my own sleeve." She shot him a playful wink. "We'll just see who wins this war."

"I thought you said it was a game," Clyde mentioned as she dropped a hot towel over his face.

"It is," she said with a wry grin. "A war game!"

CHAPTER 6

Wendy lifted her weary head from the small desk where she sat. "When will the pain go away, Lord? Please make it go away." A nagging headache had been plaguing her for hours. She was grateful her workday had finally come to an end. Her last customer, a teenager named Randy, had nearly driven her to distraction. The pimple-faced juvenile had asked for a special designer haircut with the initials *PHS* for Plumers High School cut and shaped into the back of his nearly shaven head. This took extra time of course, which meant she wasn't able to leave the shop until five thirty.

Grabbing her coat and umbrella, Wendy stepped outside. It was snowing hard. A biting wind whipped around her neck, chilling her to the bone. Caught in the current, the umbrella nearly turned inside out. With an exasperated moan, she snapped it shut. "Can anything else go wrong today?"

Wendy shivered and tromped up the snowy sidewalk toward home. Today had been such an emotional drain. First, Kyle Rogers coming in for a shave and a haircut, which had evoked all sorts of feelings she'd rather not think about. Then another 911 scare, followed by her father's admission of the false calls. After she'd returned to the shop, there had been joke-telling Clyde waiting, then several walk-ins, ending with Randy Olsen, who had just about made her crazy expecting such a ridiculous haircut! It would be so good to get out of her work clothes and into a sweat suit. After she fixed an easy supper of canned soup and grilled cheese sandwiches, she would collapse on the couch for a well-deserved rest. Hopefully, after a good night's sleep, she could come up with a game plan. She needed to figure out something that would keep Dad busy enough so he wouldn't have time to think about her needing a man.

As Wendy approached her house, she noticed there were no lights on inside. She thought that was a bit strange. Dad may not have been able to do many things, but he always managed to have several lights on in the living room.

As usual, the front door was unlocked. Wendy turned the knob and stepped inside. Everything was dark and deathly quiet. Believing Dad to still be asleep in his bedroom, she tiptoed quietly into the living room and nearly tripped over something. She bent down and snapped on a small table lamp.

Wendy let out a startled gasp as the sight of her father came into view. He was lying facedown on the floor, with one bloody hand extended over his head. "Dad! Can you hear me, Dad?" She dropped to her knees and shook his shoulder. "Dear Lord, please let him be okay."

Suddenly Dad turned his head, and

his eyes shot open. "Oh, Wendy, I'm so glad you're finally home," he rasped, attempting to roll over.

"What's wrong, Dad?" Wendy's voice shook with fear. "Why are you lying on the floor? What happened to your hand?"

"After my little stunt earlier today, I wanted to make amends," he said, wincing as she helped him roll over and then lifted his hand for inspection. "I was going to make savory stew for dinner, but I'm afraid the knife got the better of me."

"Knife?" she shrieked. "Dad, you know better than to try using a paring knife."

"Actually, it was a butcher knife," he admitted. "I couldn't get my stiff, swollen fingers to work with that little bitty thing you always use."

"So what are you doing on the floor? Did the blood loss make you dizzy?"

He struggled to sit up. "I guess maybe it did."

"Let me get a towel for that hand; then I'll help you get to the couch," Wendy said as she stood up.

"It's a pretty deep cut," her father acknowledged. "I think it might need a few stitches."

"Just stay put until I get back," she insisted.

Wendy returned with a hand towel, which she quickly wrapped around her dad's hand. "Why in the world didn't you call me, or at least call —" She stopped in midsentence. "I guess after our little discussion earlier today, you weren't about to call 911 again, right?"

"Actually, I couldn't call you or the paramedics," he replied with a scowl.

"Why not?" she asked, leaning over so she could help him stand.

"No telephone."

Her head shot up. "No phone! What are you talking about, Dad?"

He nodded toward the phone, sitting on a small table across the room. "I never even considered calling 911 this time, but I did try to call you. The phone seemed to be dead though."

Wendy led him to the couch, then moved to the telephone and picked up the receiver. She frowned. "That's funny. It was working fine when I used it earlier today." Before her father could open his mouth to comment, a light seemed to dawn. "I'll be right back."

"Where are you going?" he called to her retreating form.

"To check the extension in my room."

A few seconds later, Wendy returned to the living room, tears filling her eyes. When she knelt in front of the couch, Dad used his uninjured hand to wipe away the moisture on her cheek. "I'm gonna be okay, honey, so please don't cry."

"The phone was off the hook," she wailed. "How could I have been so careless?" She blinked several times, trying to tame the torrent of tears that seemed to keep on coming. "What if you had bled to death? What if —"

"But I didn't, and I'm going to be fine now that you're here." He gave her a reassuring smile.

"We'd better get you to the hospital. I'm sure that cut will require stitches."

"In a minute," he replied. "First I want to say something."

"What is it, Dad?"

"My actions over the past few weeks have been inexcusable, and I owe you a heartfelt apology, Wendy girl." He grimaced as though he were in pain.

She nodded. "You're forgiven."

"I made those phony calls so you could meet a nice man, but I was meddling," he acknowledged. "Matchmaking and matters of the heart should be left up to the Lord."

"You're the only man I'll ever need," Wendy said softly.

"I'm holding you back," he argued. "If you didn't have to take care of me, you'd probably be married and raising a family of your own by now. If it weren't for my disability, I'm sure you'd be going out on all kinds of dates instead of staying home and playing nurse-maid to a fully grown man."

Wendy shook her head. "I'm not interested in dating — or men, Dad."

"Why the 'I don't like men' attitude?" he pried. "You work on men's hair five days a week. I would think by now one of your customers might have caught your eye."

Wendy moaned. "Remember when I was away at barber's school?"

Her father only nodded in response.

"I dated a guy named Dale Carlson for a while. He treated me awful, Dad."

"Physical abuse?" he asked with raised eyebrows.

127

She shook her head. "No — uh — he wanted me to compromise my moral standards — if you get my meaning."

"You should have dumped that guy!"

"I didn't have to — he dumped me. When I wouldn't give in to his sexual advances, Mr. Self-Righteous, Phony Christian dropped me for Michelle Stiles."

"I guess I must have had my head in the sand," her father said in obvious surprise. "I didn't know you were that serious about anyone, much less realize some knucklehead was treating you so badly."

"I really didn't want to talk about it," Wendy admitted. "I made up my mind after the Dale fiasco that I was done with men." She shrugged. "So many of the guys who come into the barbershop are either rude, crude, or lewd."

"I understand your feelings of betrayal and hurt," her father said, "but you're not right about your interpretation of all men. One bad apple doesn't have to spoil the whole barrel, you know. You can just pluck out the rotten one and choose a Washington State Delicious."

Wendy smiled at her dad's little pun, then went to the hall closet, where she retrieved his jacket. "The roads are getting bad. I hope it won't take too long to get to the hospital."

"I don't think I'll bleed to death," he said with a sardonic smile. "If I thought it was really serious, I might have you call 911." His forehead wrinkled. "I don't think those paramedics would be too happy to get another call from here today though."

"You're probably right," she agreed. "That older guy didn't respond to you at all like Kyle Rogers, did he?"

"That's putting it mildly. I think he was more than a bit irritated with me for wasting his precious time today."

"Well, just put it out of your head," Wendy said with a smile. "Tonight, *I'm* going to be your rescuer."

The roads weren't quite as bad as Wendy expected, and they made it to the hospital in twenty minutes. Fortunately, there weren't too many emergencies that evening, so Dad was called to an examining room soon after filling out some paperwork.

"Would you like me to go along?" Wendy gave Dad's arm a little squeeze as a young nurse began to usher him away.

He shook his head. "No, I'll be fine. Why don't you go out to the waiting area and try to relax?"

Relax? How on earth was she supposed to relax when her nerves felt taut and her stomach was playing a game of leapfrog? The headache, which she'd acquired around noon, was still pulsating like a jackhammer, too. She would give anything for a cup of hot tea and an aspirin.

Wendy found a chair in the empty waiting room. She rested her elbows on her jean-clad knees and began to methodically rub her forehead. *At least Dad isn't seriously injured, and now that he's agreed to quit playing matchmaker, I don't have to rack my brain to come up with any plan to steer him in some other direction either.*

"What are *you* doing here?"

Wendy jumped at the sound of a deep male voice. Kyle Rogers stood a few feet away, smiling down at her. "Kyle! I — uh — Dad cut his hand."

"Another 911 call?" he asked with raised eyebrows.

She shook her head. "Not this time." She didn't bother telling him about the call her father had placed around noon. If the Grangely grapevine was as active as the one in her small town, then Kyle had probably already heard the whole story from the other paramedics.

"What then?" he asked, taking the seat beside her.

"Dad was trying to make supper, and the knife he was using slipped," she explained. "He has a pretty nasty

132

cut on his left thumb, and it bled quite a lot."

"It's a good thing you were home when it happened."

Wendy blinked several times. "Actually, I wasn't. He did it while I was still at work. I found him lying on the floor."

Kyle grimaced. "You drove him to the hospital yourself?"

"Of course," Wendy replied. "After today, I wasn't about to call 911."

"What happened today?"

Wendy shrugged, realizing he must not have heard anything after all. "It's not important."

She eyed him curiously. "Say, what are *you* doing here, anyway? I thought you were planning to take in a concert tonight. Shouldn't you be there and not here at the hospital?"

He chuckled. "I changed my mind about going. It didn't seem like such a good idea when I thought about attending it alone." He studied Wendy for several seconds, causing her mouth to suddenly go dry. Then he added, "I came here to check on a patient Steve and I brought in yesterday."

I wish he'd quit looking at me like that, she mused. *What are those serious brown eyes of his trying to tell me? How do I know if Kyle is really what he appears to be? I misjudged a so-called Christian once, and I —*

"It was a little boy who'd been mauled by a dog," he said, interrupting her unsettling thoughts.

"What?" Wendy shook her head and shifted restlessly in her chair, trying to force her thoughts back to what

Kyle was saying.

"The patient I came to see," he explained. "A five-year-old boy was playing at his neighbor's house and got in the middle of a cat and dog skirmish."

"How awful!" Wendy exclaimed. "Is he going to be all right?"

Kyle nodded. "He'll probably undergo extensive plastic surgery, but I think the little tyke will be fine."

"It's — uh — thoughtful of you to care so much about the patients you bring to the hospital," she stammered. "I think you go over and above the call of duty as a paramedic."

In a surprise gesture, Kyle reached for Wendy's hand. "I do care about my patients, but I also care about you and your father. In fact, I've been thinking that I might stop in and see you both from time to time — when I'm not on duty, that is."

She swallowed hard. "You've been thinking that?"

He nodded. "I really believe your dad could use some company, and since you're so opposed to me playing matchmaker —"

"Don't even go there," she warned.

He shrugged. "Okay, but I could sure use a good barber."

She pulled her hand sharply away. *So that's all he sees me as — just a good barber. In spite of my misgivings, I was actually beginning to think — hope, really — that Kyle was interested in me as a woman, and not merely someone to give him a shave and a haircut. I knew Mr. Perfect Paramedic was too good to be true. He's probably no different than Dale or Gabe after all.*

Just when I'm beginning to make a bit of headway, Wendy pulls into her shell, Kyle thought, letting his head drop into his hands. *What's it going to take to break down her wall of mistrust and get her to open up to me?*

"Dad thinks you're perfect, you know," Wendy blurted out, interrupting his thoughts. "He wants us to get married."

Kyle's head jerked up. "What? Your dad wants *what?*"

"He tried to set us up." Wendy's face contorted. "That's why Dad kept calling 911."

Kyle chewed thoughtfully on his lower lip. "All the calls were phony?"

She nodded. "Every last one of

them. He even made a third call around noon today, saying something about feeling dizzy. I thought you might have heard about that one."

He shook his head. "No, I didn't. How do you know he was faking it?"

"He admitted it," she said. "After Steve and Phil left this afternoon, Dad confessed that he'd been trying to play matchmaker all along."

Kyle sucked in a deep breath and expelled it with force. "But today was my day off. I didn't even respond to his 911 call, so —"

"I know," she interrupted. "He was really upset when you didn't show up. That's when I began to get suspicious. Up until then, I just thought he was trying to get attention or simply needed someone to talk to."

Kyle mopped his forehead with the

back of his shirtsleeve. "Whew! This is pretty heavy stuff."

She nodded. "My feelings exactly!"

"And here I was trying to come up with some way to fix your dad up with Edna Stone." Kyle shook his head slowly. "Wayne was one step ahead of me all the way, wasn't he?"

"Dad's a pretty slick operator, all right," Wendy admitted. "Guess that's why he did well in business for so many years."

Kyle's eyebrows shot up. "Are you saying that Wayne was dishonest in his business dealings?"

Wendy waved one hand in the air. "No, no, of course not. I just meant —"

"You can see your father now, Miss Campbell," a woman's soft voice interrupted.

Kyle and Wendy both turned to face the nurse who had just entered the waiting room. "Would you like me to go with you?" Kyle asked.

Wendy shook her head. "No, thanks. Dad's my problem, not yours." She stood up and left the room before Kyle could say another word.

"Oh Lord, what have I gotten myself into?" he moaned.

CHAPTER 7

Over the next several weeks, some drastic changes were made at the Campbell house. Dad no longer spent his time playing matchmaker, which was a welcome relief for Wendy. She was sure it had taken a lot of energy for him to scheme and make those false 911 calls. Even though he'd done it out of love and concern for her, she was glad that whole scenario was behind them. Wendy still got goose bumps every time she heard a siren, but she felt a small sense of peace knowing that if the ambulance should ever go to her house again, it would be for a "real" emergency and not some trumped-up illness.

Another change, which was definitely for the better, was the fact that Dad had asked to go to church again. Wendy, wanting to please her father, was willing to accompany him. She hadn't completely dealt with her feelings of mistrust or self-doubt, but at least she was being exposed to the Word of God each week. That fact made her feel somewhat better about herself and her circumstances.

True to his word, Kyle Rogers had become a regular visitor, both at the Campbell home and at Wendy's barbershop. A few times Kyle had taken Dad out for a ride in his Bronco and had even made a commitment to see that he would go fishing in the spring — with or without Edna Stone.

"There's no reason your dad can't keep on doing some fun things," Kyle informed Wendy when he stopped by the barbershop one afternoon.

"I doubt that he could even bait his line, much less catch any fish."

"He doesn't have to," Kyle asserted. "I'll do everything for him, and all he will have to do is just sit in a folding chair and hold the pole."

If another customer hadn't come in, Wendy might have debated further. Instead she merely shrugged. "Spring is still a few months away. When the time comes, we'll talk about it."

Kyle flashed her a grin and sauntered out the door.

Wendy frowned. She found his

warm smile and kind words unnerving — right along with the verses of scripture he'd quoted on his last few visits. One verse in particular had really set her to thinking. It was Proverbs 29: 25: *"Fear of man will prove to be a snare, but whoever trusts in the Lord is kept safe."* Wendy's trust hadn't been in the Lord for a long time. She wasn't sure she could ever trust again. After the loss of her mother, her father being diagnosed with crippling arthritis, then the episode with Dale, how could she have faith in anyone or anything?

There was also the matter of all the crude, rude men and boys who came into her barbershop. She wasn't a "perfect" Christian by any means, but it was difficult to look past all these men's bad habits and sometimes downright sinful ways. How could she ever believe that any man, except for Dad, could be kind and loving?

"Hey, Wendy, are ya gonna cut my hair or not?"

Jerking her thoughts back to the job at hand, Wendy turned toward the barber's chair. Gabe Hunter was eyeing her curiously. It had only been a few weeks, but the egotistic Romeo was back for another haircut.

He probably came in just to bug me, she grumbled silently. *Well, this time I refuse to let him ruffle my feathers. If he thinks he even has half a chance with me, he's in for a rude awakening!*

Kyle left Wendy's shop feeling more confused than he had in weeks. She seemed interested in the scriptures he'd been sharing with her, and on one occasion had even told him that she and her dad were going to church again. That should have had him singing God's praises. It had been his desire to help both Wendy and Wayne find their way back to the Lord. In a roundabout way, he'd accomplished that, too.

"Then why am I feeling so down?" he vocalized as he headed toward his Bronco.

"You're lonely, Kyle," a little voice nudged. *"You've convinced yourself that there is no room for love or romance in your heart. You're not trusting Me in all areas of your life either."*

"What do you want me to do, Lord — ask Wendy on a date?"

No answer. That still, small voice seemed to have vanished as quickly as it had come. Kyle scratched the back of his head and grimaced. He needed time to think. He needed time to pray about this. A drive up to Plumers Pond sure seemed to be in order.

"You've got a phone call," Dad announced as he hobbled into the kitchen where Wendy was cooking.

"Who is it? Can you take a message? Supper's almost ready, and —"

"It's Kyle," her father said with a smirk.

Wendy turned the stove down, put a lid on the spaghetti sauce, and headed for the living room. "Hello, Kyle," she said into the phone. "What's up?"

"I — uh," Kyle stammered.

"You sound kind of nervous."

"Yeah, I guess I am."

"Well, you needn't be. I don't bite, you know." She chuckled. "Some of my customers might think I am pretty *cutting,* though."

Kyle laughed at her pun, which seemed to put him at ease. "Listen, the reason I'm calling is, I was up at Plumers Pond today, and it's still frozen solid."

"I'm not surprised," Wendy replied. "It's been a drawn-out, cold winter, and I'm beginning to wonder if spring will ever get here." There was a long pause, which left her wondering if maybe Kyle had hung up. "Are you still there, Kyle?"

"Yeah, I'm here," he said with a small laugh. "I was just trying to get up enough nerve to ask if you'd like to go ice-skating with me on Saturday night."

"Ice-skating?" she echoed.

"I just found out that the singles' group from my church is going out to the pond for a skating party. I thought it might be kind of fun, and I'd really like it if you went along."

Wendy's mind whirled. Was this a date he was asking her on? Not Kyle dropping by the barbershop for a short visit. Not Dad and her going to a Christian concert — but just the two of them, skating with a bunch of other people their own age. She did enjoy Kyle's company; there was no denying it. In all the times she'd seen him, he'd never once said an unkind thing or done anything to make her think he was anything less than the Christian he professed to be. Still —

"Now it's my turn to ask. Are you

there?" Kyle's deep voice cut into her troubling thoughts.

"Yes, I'm here," she said in a trembling voice. "I was just taken by surprise, that's all."

"Surprised that I ice-skate, or that I'm asking you out on a date?"

So it was a real date then. Kyle had just said as much. Now her only problem was deciding whether to accept or not. Wendy hadn't been on a date since she and Dale broke up. Could she really start dating after all this time? Could she trust Kyle not to break her heart the way Dale had? Of course, that could easily be avoided by simply not allowing herself to become romantically involved again.

"How about it, Wendy?" Kyle asked, invading her thoughts once more.

"Can I pick you up around seven Saturday evening?"

Wendy licked her lips and swallowed hard. She opened her mouth to decline, but to her surprise, she said, "Sure, why not?"

"Great!" Kyle said enthusiastically. "See you soon."

Wendy hung up the phone and dropped onto the couch with a groan. "Now why in the world did I say yes?"

Being with Kyle and the other young people turned out to be more fun than Wendy expected.

"You're a good skater," Kyle said, skidding to a stop in front of Wendy, nearly causing her to lose her balance.

"You're not so bad yourself," she

shot back.

"Are you having fun?" He pivoted so he could skate beside her.

She nodded. "It's been years since I've been on skates. I wasn't sure I could even stand up on these skinny little blades, much less make it all the way around the frozen pond."

"How about taking a break?" Kyle suggested. "One of the guys has started a bonfire. We've got lots of hot dogs and marshmallows to roast."

"I admit, I am kind of hungry. Guess all this cold, fresh air has given me an appetite."

"Yeah, me, too. Of course, I could eat anytime. While I was growing up in Northern California, Mom used to say all three of us boys could eat her out of house and home."

Wendy giggled. "So is a voracious

appetite your worst sin?"

He eyed her curiously. "You're kidding, right?"

She shook her head and reached up to slip her fuzzy blue earmuffs back in place. "You seem so nice — almost perfect. Dad thinks you're about the best thing to happen since the invention of homemade ice cream."

"Whoa!" Kyle raised one gloved hand. "I don't even come close to being perfect. I may strive to be more like Jesus; but like any other human being, perfectionism is something I'll sure never know."

Wendy shrugged. "Maybe I expect too much from people. Dad says I do anyway."

"Part of living the Christian life is being willing to accept others just as they are, Wendy."

Kyle reached for her hand.

Even though they both wore gloves, she could feel the warmth of his touch. It caused her heart to skip a few beats. Kyle's serious, dark eyes seemed to be challenging her to let go of the past and forgive those who had hurt her. She wanted so badly to believe Kyle was different from Dale or any of the guys who came into the barbershop, wanting more than she was willing to give. How good it would feel to accept folks for who they were and quit looking for perfection. Most importantly, Wendy would have to learn to trust again, and that frightened her. She might be able to trust the Lord, but trusting another man would put her in a vulnerable position. Wendy wasn't sure she could risk being hurt again.

The ride back to town was a quiet one. Both Wendy and Kyle seemed absorbed in their own private thoughts. Only the pleasant strain of Steve Green's mellow voice singing "My Soul Found Rest" filled the interior of Kyle's Bronco. Wendy struggled with tears that threatened to spill over. She wondered if her soul would ever find rest amid the turmoil of life.

"This is my favorite CD," Kyle said, breaking the silence between them. "Steve Green has so many good songs. I always feel as though the Lord is speaking to my heart when I listen to contemporary Christian music."

Wendy could only nod. She didn't

want to admit it to Kyle, but she rarely ever listened to any type of music. In fact, some music actually grated on her nerves, but the song that played now had a serene effect on her. She was beginning to think maybe she should start playing some Christian music in her shop. *That might even deter some of the crude lumberjacks from telling all their lewd jokes and wisecracks,* she mused.

"I'll bet someone could even get saved listening to Christian music like what's on this CD," Wendy said, hardly realizing she'd spoken her thoughts out loud.

"I think you're right," Kyle agreed. "In fact, some of the teens at my church found Christ at a Christian rock concert not so long ago."

Wendy frowned. "I've been a Christian since I was a child, but I strayed from God a few years ago." She had absolutely no idea why she was telling Kyle all this, but the words seemed to keep tumbling out. "After a bad relationship with a so-called Christian, I was terribly hurt and started to get bitter about certain things." When Kyle remained quiet, she added solemnly, "God could have kept it from happening, you know."

"God doesn't always make things go away just so we will have it easy," Kyle put in. "Part of growing in our Christian walk is learning how to cope with life's problems and letting Christ carry our burdens when the load is too heavy for us."

"I don't do too well in the trusting department either," Wendy admitted, leaning back in the seat and closing her eyes.

"Who don't you trust?" Kyle glanced over at her with a look of concern.

"Men," she announced. "I don't trust men."

Kyle's forehead wrinkled. "Not even your dad?"

She opened her eyes and shrugged. "Until he started making false 911 calls, I had always trusted Dad implicitly."

"But he really feels bad about all that and has promised it will never happen again," Kyle reminded. "Just last week, when I took him for a ride up to Plumers Creek, Wayne told me how guilty he felt for telling all those lies." He reached over to pat Wendy's hand. "Your dad's a Christian, but he's not perfect either. Like I was telling you earlier tonight, we all make mistakes. It's what we do about our blunders that really counts."

"I think I can trust Dad again," Wendy said thoughtfully. "It's other men that give me a problem."

Kyle grew serious. "Other men, like me?"

She laughed nervously. "You get paid to be trustworthy."

"I'm not always working though," he reminded. "I have to try to be a Christian example whether I'm administering first aid to an accident victim or teaching a sixth-grade Sunday school class full of unruly boys."

"You teach Sunday school?" she asked in surprise.

He nodded. "Yep, every other week — on the Sundays when I'm not scheduled for duty. Sometimes those rowdy kids are enough to put any-one's Christianity to the test."

Wendy thought about the hyperac-tive, undisciplined kids who came into the barbershop. They needed to be shown the love of Jesus, too. There had to be a better way to deal with her customers than merely pretend-ing to be friendly, or snapping back at guys like Gabe. At that moment, Wendy resolved in her heart to find out what it was.

CHAPTER 8

Wendy brought her Bible to the shop to read during lulls. If she was going to find a better way to deal with the irritation she felt with some of her customers, she knew the answer would be found in the scriptures. She also planned to buy a few Christian CDs so she could play them at work — both for her own benefit as well as the clientele's.

Today was a cold, blustery Tuesday, and she'd only had two customers so far. She didn't really mind though, because it was another opportunity to get into God's Word. She grabbed an apple from the fruit bowl on the counter, dropped into her barber's chair, and randomly opened the Bible to the book of Matthew.

Chapter 7 dealt with the subject of judging others. Wendy was reminded that instead of searching for sawdust in someone else's eyes, she should be examining her own life and looking for the plank that would no doubt be there, in the form of her own sin. She chewed thoughtfully on the Red Delicious apple and let the Holy Spirit speak to her heart. Instead of enjoying the unique variety of people who frequented her shop, she'd been judging them. Rather than allowing herself to get a kick out of the clean jokes and witnessing about the Lord to those who told off-color puns, she'd been telling herself that all men were bad. Even though Kyle Rogers had made an impression on her with his tenderness, patience, and kind words, Wendy had questioned his motives. This was judging. There was no getting around it, and according to God's Word, Wendy was no better than the worst of all sinners. If she didn't get herself right with the Lord, she, too, would be judged.

Without a moment's hesitation, she knew what she must do. Wendy bowed her head and prayed fervently, "Father, please forgive me for my negative, condemning attitude. Heal me of the hurt deep in my heart, and help me learn to love others just as You do. Help me to trust You and become a witness of Your love and grace." A small sob escaped her lips.

"And if Kyle Rogers is the man you want me to love and trust, then please give me some sign." When she finished her heartfelt prayer, Wendy opened her eyes. For the first time since her broken relationship with Dale Carlson, she felt a sense of peace flood her soul. She was released from all the pain of the past and knew that with God's help, she could finally be a witness for Him.

Wendy glanced out the front window and caught sight of Harvey, the mailman, slipping some mail into the box outside the shop. She stepped down from the chair. Taking one more bite of the crisp, juicy apple, she headed outside, not even bothering with a coat.

Kyle was just rounding the corner,

heading up the street toward Campbell's Barbershop, when he saw Wendy come out the front door. His mouth curved into a smile. He hadn't seen her since their date last Saturday night. He could only hope that she'd be as glad to see him as he was to see her now.

Kyle had spent most of the weekend thinking about Wendy and the way she made him feel. His resolve not to get romantically involved with any woman was quickly fading, and he seemed powerless to stop it. He'd read the scriptures and prayed until there were no more words. He'd petitioned God to show him some sign that Wendy might be able to respond to his love. He didn't have a clue what it might be, but just the same, he'd made up his mind to come to the shop today and have a heart-to-heart talk with Wendy. If she would agree to at least give their relationship a chance, then he was going to trust God to work out all the details that seemed impossible to him. After all, if he was really trying to do the things Jesus would do, it wasn't his right to make decisions about the future. Fear that his job would get in the way of love or marriage could no longer be an issue.

Kyle watched in fascination as petite little Wendy, wearing only a pair of blue jeans and a long-sleeved blouse, covered with a green smock, reached into the mailbox. It was a cold day, and there was still snow on the ground. The sidewalk appeared slick, like the frozen pond, with ice glistening in the sun's golden rays.

Kyle was about to call out for her to be careful when the unthinkable happened. Just like an ice skater who'd lost her balance, Wendy's body swayed first to one side, then the other. Her feet slipped and slid while she tried hopelessly to regain her balance. There seemed to be nothing Kyle could do but stand there and watch as beautiful little Wendy went down, landing hard on her back and hitting her head against the icy, cold sidewalk.

Doing a fair share of slipping and sliding himself, Kyle raced down the sidewalk to Wendy's aid. When he discovered that she wasn't conscious, his paramedic skills kicked in. From the evidence of the apple core lying nearby, Kyle was quite sure Wendy not only had the wind knocked out of her, but was probably asphyxiating on a piece of that apple. He knew what he had to do, and it must be done quickly, or she would choke to death.

Kyle positioned her head and knelt closer. *Look, listen, feel for air. . . .* His training ran through his mind.

Nothing!

He repositioned her jaw again, but to no avail. When he tried to give her mouth-to-mouth, it didn't work. Everything confirmed his worst suspicions: a small piece of the offending fruit must be stuck in her throat. He went into immediate action and was able to dislodge it using the Heimlich maneuver. His initial burst of praise and elation faded at once when Wendy still didn't breathe on her own. Fearful for her life, yet relying on his faith, he began mouth-to-mouth resuscitation again.

Breathe, Wendy honey. . . . God, please make her breathe. . . .

Though she started breathing, she still didn't regain consciousness. "Wake up, beautiful lady. I haven't told you what I came to say." Kyle quickly examined her to be sure nothing was injured. He prayed earnestly, "Oh Lord, this is not the way I planned for things to be. I had a whole speech prepared for Wendy, and now I may never get the chance to say what's on my mind. Please, Lord — let her be all right."

Wendy's eyelids popped open. Someone's lips had been touching hers. They were soft and warm. She thought she'd heard a voice. Had someone called her *beautiful?* Kyle stared down at her with a look of love and concern etched on his handsome face. Where was she, and why was he leaning over her? She was sure she must be dreaming.

"Wh–what happened?"

"I was coming to your shop so I could talk to you about something very important," Kyle explained, gently stroking the side of her face. He leaned closer and kissed her forehead, his tears falling to her cheeks. "I saw you slip and fall on the ice. You choked on that apple." He pointed to the small piece, just a few feet away. "Thank God you're alive!"

"I was just finishing the apple when I walked outside to get the mail. I — I —"

Kyle placed one finger against her lips. "Shh . . . Don't try to talk right now." He probed the back of her head gently with his fingers. "As amazing as this may seem, there's not even a lump. Does your head hurt anywhere?"

She smiled up at him, tears gathering in her own eyes. "No, not really. I think I just had the wind knocked out of me."

"You looked so helpless and beautiful — just like Snow White, lying there beside that Red Delicious," Kyle said with a catch in his voice. "Only your apple wasn't poison, and I thank God you responded to the Heimlich maneuver, then mouth-to-mouth resuscitation so quickly."

"Mouth-to-mouth?" she echoed, bringing her fingers up to lightly touch her lips. "At first I thought I was dreaming. Then I opened my eyes and thought I'd been kissed by a very handsome man." A shiver ran up her spine, and she knew it was not from the cold. "And you must be Prince Charming, who came along and rescued me."

He nodded. "I know God sent me here today, but I sure didn't think I'd be playing the part of a paramedic on my day off."

She smiled up at him. "You've rescued me from a whole lot more than a fall to the ice and an apple stuck in my throat."

"Really? What else have I rescued you from?" Kyle asked, never taking his eyes off her smiling face.

She swallowed hard. "Your kindness, patience, and biblical counseling have all helped. I was reading my Bible right before I came outside, and God's Word confirmed everything you've been trying to tell me."

"I'm so glad," he said sincerely.

"Thanks for saving me," she whispered as she sat up. "I — I probably shouldn't be saying this, but I think I might be falling in love with you."

"You took the words right out of my mouth." He bent his head down to capture her mouth in a kiss so sweet it took her breath away.

"Oh, Kyle," she murmured when their lips finally separated, "if you keep that up, I might be forced to call 911."

He laughed heartily. "Guess I'd better get you inside to the phone, then, because now that God has finally kicked some sense into my stubborn head, I'm liable to keep kissing you all day long."

Wendy drew in a deep breath and leaned her head against his strong shoulder. As they entered the barbershop a few moments later, she murmured, "Thank You, Lord. I think I can learn to trust both You and Kyle now." Her flushed cheeks dimpled as she smiled. "And thank you, Dad — our matchmaker 911."

ABOUT THE AUTHOR

Wanda E. Brunstetter is a bestselling author who enjoys writing Amish-themed as well as contemporary and historical novels. Descended from Anabaptists herself, Wanda became deeply interested in the Plain People when she married her husband, Richard, who grew up in a Mennonite church in Pennsylvania. Wanda and her husband live in Washington State but take every opportunity to visit their Amish friends in various communities across the country, gathering further information about the Amish way of life.

Wanda and her husband have two grown children and six grand-children. In her spare time, Wanda enjoys photography, ventriloquism, gardening, reading, stamping, and having fun with her family.

In addition to her novels, Wanda has written Amish cookbooks, Amish devotionals, and several Amish children's books as well as numerous novellas, stories, articles, poems, and puppet scripts.

Visit Wanda's website at www.wandabrunstetter.com and feel free to e-mail her at wanda@wandabrunstetter.com.

The employees of Thorndike Press hope you have enjoyed this Large Print book. All our Thorndike, Wheeler, and Kennebec Large Print titles are designed for easy reading, and all our books are made to last. Other Thorndike Press Large Print books are available at your library, through selected bookstores, or directly from us.

For information about titles, please call:
  (800) 223-1244

or visit our Web site at:
  http://gale.cengage.com/thorndike

To share your comments, please write:
  Publisher
  Thorndike Press
  10 Water St., Suite 310
  Waterville, ME 04901